The New Series

The Bully

a novel

by

LIZ BROWN

H·I·P Books

New Series Canada

Copyright © 2005 by High Interest Publishing

Library and Archives Canada Cataloguing in Publication

Brown, Liz, 1981–
      The bully / Liz Brown.

(New Series Canada)
ISBN 1-897039-08-5

I. Title. II. Series.

PS8603.R685B84 2005   jC813'.6   C2005-900837-7

General editor: Paul Kropp
Text design: Laura Brady
Illustrations drawn by: Catherinr Doherty
Cover design: Robert Corrigan

1 2 3 4 5 6 7   07 06 05 04 03 02

Printed and bound in Canada

High Interest Publishing is an imprint of the Chestnut Publishing Group

Sugar and spice and everything . . .
mean. Allie finds that the worst bully
at her school is a girl, and the worst
weapon can be a whisper.

CHAPTER 1

Sugar and Spice

Sugar and spice and everything nice
That's what little girls are made of . . .

The person who wrote that dumb old poem never met Danni Heller. If the poet had met her, the lines would be way different. *Vinegar and cotton and everything rotten. That's what Danni Heller is made of.*

For a long time, I thought Danni Heller was

gone for good. I hadn't seen her since Grade 8. I figured she was just a bad memory that would some day fade away.

But then Danni came back into my life, big time.

It started back in April when a bunch of us were waiting in line to go to a movie. I was with my boyfriend, Justin. He's one of the cutest guys in school. He's tall, dark and handsome — really, he is. He always seemed too cool to be going out with a girl like me. But we'd been seeing each other for six months now, and we spent a lot of time together.

Justin and I were standing in line when his cell phone rang. He looked down, saw the number, and cut it off.

"Who was that?" I asked him. I wasn't being nosy — really, I wasn't. I was just kind of curious.

But then Justin turned red in the face. "Just some stupid girl," he said, "bugging me."

"Anybody I know?" I asked him.

"Don't think so," he replied. "I think her name is Danielle something . . . I can't remember the last name."

Suddenly I felt myself turn red in the face. "Danni Heller?" I asked.

"Yeah, that's her name," he said, almost with a shrug. "Doesn't know how to take *no* for an answer, I guess."

Then he kissed me on the cheek and the line began to move into the theatre. I couldn't ask him any more questions then. Nor could he sense the awful beating of my heart.

When I got home that night, I phoned my best friend Caitlin right away. I told her about the phone call — or maybe I should say the phone calls.

"The whole time we were in the movie, Danni kept calling Justin's cell phone." I got mad just thinking about it.

"Ohmygod," Caitlin said. I bet she was rolling her eyes as she sat in her bedroom. "I thought she moved away, like four years ago."

"Danni is like that guy Freddie in the horror movies — she's back," I groaned.

"Doesn't she get the message? Can't she see that Justin doesn't want her."

"Guess not," I replied. "The problem is, Justin

kind of likes the way some girls chase after him. I mean, Danni always dressed in tight clothes back in Grade 8. I can just imagine what she wears now."

"Why would Justin look at her when he's got you?" said Caitlin.

"I don't think he's looking," I sighed. "At least not now."

"You sure?" Caitlin asked. "Somehow she got his cell number."

"Well, we've had a few problems," I admitted. "I mean, there are some things I just won't do for him. You know what I mean. And Justin is a guy. I mean, all guys are out for what they can get."

Now it was Caitlin's turn to sigh. She's been dumped by more than one guy for saying the word *no*.

"But, Allie, you're so great! You're smart and talented and cute. I don't think you have to worry about somebody like Danni Heller."

I smiled. Caitlin was my best friend and I knew she was just trying to make me feel better. Danni Heller wasn't a threat to me, I thought.

When I last saw Danni, she was pretty good looking in a trashy kind of way. She started getting boobs before the rest of us and was pretty big even in Grade 8. Back then she wore her tops tight, just to show off. She wore her skirts short even if her legs weren't great. She looked hot, as the guys would say.

Me? I was a little on the short side. I've got frizzy brown hair and a skinny body with no real shape. But I'm smart and funny and nice to be with, I think. Guys don't just care about how a girl looks, do they?

I was thinking about all that the next morning, at my locker. Caitlin was right beside me since we traded to get our lockers together.

"Here comes your guy," said Caitlin, breaking into my thoughts.

And there he was, smiling and towering over me. Justin is well over six feet tall and plays forward on the basketball team. I have to crane my neck just to look up into his face.

"Hey, Allie," Justin said, giving me a quick peck on the forehead. If you tried to do a real kiss in our high school, the teachers would be down on you in a second.

Caitlin turned to Justin. "So I hear you have a new admirer," she joked.

"Who told you that," he said, glaring back at her.

"Uh . . . nobody," Caitlin stammered, then grabbed her books. "It's just a rumour. Look, Allie, I gotta get to class, see you later!"

"Sure," I said, but Caitlin was already rushing down the hall.

Justin and I were left standing there, both feeling awkward.

"Why'd you get mad at Caitlin?" I asked, since he really had no reason to.

"Why are you telling people about that girl?" Justin asked. "Maybe Danni's just trying to be friendly. What's so bad about that?"

"I guess if that's what you want." I said, slamming my locker shut.

I was trying to stay cool, trying to keep my temper under control. I didn't *own* Justin just because he was my boyfriend. I couldn't tell him which kids he could e-mail, or whom he could call on the phone. But that didn't mean I was happy with Danni and her moves.

Then I heard Danni's voice from down the hall.

"Hey, Justin, you're looking hot today," she said, strolling up to my boyfriend.

The tone of her voice sounded like some hooker in a TV movie. When I turned, I saw that Danni had dressed to suit the voice. She was wearing a short, short skirt and a top that was two sizes too small. Her makeup was done perfectly, but it was way too heavy. She looked like she was about to go to a nightclub, not homeroom.

Justin just grinned and stared at her.

Then Danni turned to me and sneered. "Too bad your girl doesn't look as hot as you do, Justin," she cooed. "You could do better, you know."

I couldn't believe it. This tramp was coming on to my boyfriend — and cutting me down — right in front of my face.

I crossed my arms and glared back at her. I kept waiting for Justin to stick up for me, to tell Danni to leave him alone. But he just stood there and let

out a little laugh. He thought it was all some kind of joke!

"I guess I'll see you later," said Danni, smiling at Justin.

Justin watched her walk all the way down the hall, his eyes all over her.

That's when I got really angry. *Livid* — that's a vocabulary word in English class — I got livid.

"I can't believe you just laughed at all that!" I snapped at him. "Are you my boyfriend or what? You're supposed to stand up for me, not laugh at stuff like that," I said, spitting out the words.

"Allie, you need to calm down," Justin replied. "It was just a joke. I don't know why you have to be so jealous all the time. Just because a girl comes on to me doesn't mean I want to date her."

"I'm not jealous," I snapped back. "But I get kind of mad when my own boyfriend won't stick up for me."

"Sorry, Allie," he laughed, kissing my forehead again. "I'll let people know that my girlfriend doesn't like kidding around," Justin told me.

Just then the buzzer rang. I grabbed my books and started walking down the hall. I pretended not to care. I pretended to be cool and under control. But I could already feel tears running down my cheeks. It wasn't fair, I thought.

Danni Heller had come back to ruin my life. And this would be the second time she'd done it.

CHAPTER 2

That Was Then, This Is Worse

Danni began to bully me back in Grade 7. That was four years ago. It still gives me shivers when I think back. Danni Heller was the worst bully in our school — and she was a girl.

You read about *boy* bullies all the time. Your hear how they choose a victim. How they choose some kid who's smaller and weaker than they are. You hear how they pick on the kid, day after day.

You hear about all the physical stuff — the pushes, the punches, the kicks.

But girl bullies aren't like that. A girl bully won't beat you up. A girl bully won't push you up against a schoolyard fence. A girl bully doesn't do that much physical stuff. Instead, she beats up your brain. She makes you so scared that you wake up each day just ready to cry.

I know — I was the victim. Danielle Heller was the bully.

It didn't make sense when it all started. Danni and I had been best friends when we were little, but then things got messed up. It wasn't even her fault. Danni's stepdad got thrown in jail for robbing a gas station. After that it didn't seem like Danni cared about school . . . or much of anything. She started hanging out with tougher, older kids at school. I heard she took up smoking and drinking, way back when she was still a kid.

Of course, my life had changed, too. Caitlin moved in across the street, and she was a lot more fun to be with. We played tennis and told jokes and read the same books. Danni moved off to a

new group of kids. Caitlin and I became best friends.

Maybe Danni didn't like that. Maybe she was jealous when Caitlin became my friend. Maybe she thought that Caitlin and I looked down on her — that we were stuck up. Or maybe I'm just blaming myself. They say that victims do that. We blame ourselves for what the bully does.

The problem between Danni and me really started at school. We were in the girls' bathroom with our new lipsticks, trying to look "beautiful." Then Danni took her lipstick and wrote a couple of swear words on the walls. She started laughing. It was like the swear words were the biggest joke in the world. I told her to cut it out because I didn't want to get in trouble. Then Danny put a big streak of lipstick on my cheek. I couldn't believe it! She had this strange look on her face. It was like she was angry at me or proud of herself, or something.

So I ran out, rubbing the mark off with a tissue.

I knew that Danni was having trouble at home. I knew she was hanging out with a tough crowd. So I didn't blame her, that day. I didn't tell our teacher, or anyone, what had happened.

But Danni still got caught. I think the principal knew who did it all along. I know he called me into the office, but I kept my mouth shut. I'm not a rat — really, I'm not. But somehow Danni got nailed for the mess. She was suspended for a few days, and then it got worse. Her mom kicked her out of her house for a week.

When Danni came back to school, she blamed me. She said that I was a rat. She said I was the *only* one who could have told on her. And the word began to spread. We weren't friends any more, and I was a rat.

When we all came back to Grade 8, I thought it would be over. I thought that Danni would forget over the summer. But I was so wrong! Grade 8 was the year Danni turned mean. It was all little stuff — a note passed in class, a nasty word, a mean look on her face. I was being bullied, but no one could see it.

My friend Caitlin said I was too sensitive. She said I should ignore all the stuff. But I couldn't. Danni had been my friend, and now she was making trouble for me. She kept it up, day after day. It kept on until Christmas — and then Danni was gone.

Nobody knew where Danni had gone. The word was that her mom and stepdad broke up. Some kids said that Danni had to move with her mom. But other kids said that Danni had been kicked out again, for good. Nobody knew for sure.

But nobody was as glad as I was. My life got back to normal. I could stop looking over my shoulder. I could walk down the hall or head to the bathroom without worrying. I became the normal, happy kid I used to be.

Until Danni came back. Until Danni came back to mess up my life again.

*   *   *

I felt better when the last buzzer rang at school. All day I had been mad at Justin. I did my best to avoid him. At lunch I saw him waiting for me at my locker, so I turned and walked to the pizza place next door. I grabbed a slice of pizza and ate by myself. I didn't want to talk to him. I didn't want to get into another fight.

I guess I didn't feel like talking to anyone. At the end of classes, I grabbed my stuff and walked out the school's back door. I would have met Caitlin, but she was at a soccer practice. That left me walking home by myself.

I didn't get that far. Danni was waiting at the street that led to my house. I thought about turning back. I could pretend that I'd forgotten something at school. But that would just make it worse. If she was going to do something, I might as well face it.

"Well, if it isn't the rat," Danni said, as I came close.

"Hello, Danni," I said, trying to keep cool.

I wanted to keep walking, to get home, but Danni stepped in front of me.

"I hear you've got your claws into Justin," she said.

"He's my boyfriend," I said.

"For now," Danni told me, her tone carrying the threat. "Maybe he's your boyfriend *for now*, but things can change just like . . . " and then she snapped her fingers.

"Not Justin," I said.

"Yeah, you just keep hoping," Danni snapped back. "I know what guys like, Allie, even nice boys like Justin."

I didn't want to hear any more. I pushed past her and walked quickly down the street.

Danni shouted after me. "Next time you kiss him, Allie, make it a good one. Because you'll be kissing him goodbye."

CHAPTER 3

It Can't Hurt to Be Nice

When I came through the door, I could smell my mom's cooking. "Is that you, Allie?" she shouted from the kitchen.

"Yeah it's me," I sighed. I was hoping my mom wouldn't be home from work yet. I needed some time to myself, just to settle down.

It was that old feeling inside me. It was exactly the way I felt back in Grade 8. Danni was beating me up, inside, in my head. She was threatening —

pushing into my life. She was making me feel scared and miserable.

"Could you give me a hand with dinner? Your dad's working late and your brother's at a friend's house."

"Yeah, I guess," I said. I threw my backpack down at the door and went to the kitchen.

"Are you feeling okay," asked my mom "Did you have a bad day at school?"

"I don't want to talk about it," I snapped.

"Is it that Justin boy?" my mom asked.

I just shrugged. My mom didn't like my going out with Justin. He was my first boyfriend, ever, and mom thought I wasn't ready yet. She still wanted me to be her little girl, to play with dolls and ride my bike. But I was ready for Justin, really I was. Sometimes he wanted to go a little too far, but that's what boys are like. Isn't it?

At one point, I grabbed a potato and started to peel it. I pretended that the potato was Danni. *Take that*, I said to myself, cutting off some skin. *Take that*.

Then I felt guilty about my own thoughts. It was

bad enough that I snapped at my mom, but now I was going nuts with a potato. *Cool it,* I told myself, *or you'll be as bad as Danni is.*

After dinner, I grabbed my backpack and went upstairs. I figured that doing my math homework would help get my mind off everything. When that was done, I told myself, I would call Justin. It wasn't that I was scared by what Danni had said, but that we needed to talk.

I had just finished my last math problem and had closed the book when the phone rang.

"Hello?" I said, picking up the phone in my room.

"Allie?" It was Justin. I felt angry, relieved, upset, happy, romantic and scared — all at once.

"Oh, Justin," I sighed.

"Look, I'm sorry about today," he began.

"Today was all just a mistake," I told him. "It was a bad dream that won't happen again. I promise."

"I'm with you, Allie. I should have told Danni to disappear. Nothing like that will happen again. I promise."

"She's going to make moves on you," I said.

"Well, I can do better than that little tramp. I've got you, Allie. I don't need anybody else."

It was one of those phone calls you see in the movies — all soft focus and nice music. Justin told me how nice I was, how pretty, how sweet. And I lapped up every word. I told him how important he was to me, how much I cared about him. And we made promises to each other. We made promises that should have stopped Danni Heller right in her tracks.

After I got off the phone with him, I called Caitlin. It was one thing to get promises, but I needed some advice. Caitlin would know what to do.

"Allie? How come your line's been busy?" Caitlin asked when she answered the phone.

"I was talking to Justin," I explained. "We had kind of a fight over Danni and had to make up. But you'll never guess what happened at school!"

"Tell me everything!" she cried.

"Danni came by after you left and made some sleazy moves on Justin. Then she said a couple nasty things to me. Justin was right there and laughed like it was all a joke!"

"Guys are jerks!" said Caitlin.

"But then it got worse on the way home," I told her. "You'll never guess who was waiting for me."

"Danni Heller."

"Yeah," I said, "and she . . . she. . ." I couldn't get the words out. Somehow tears were coming to my eyes and I couldn't even speak.

"Did she threaten you, or what?" Caitlin asked.

Finally I got some control back. "She said that I should kiss Justin goodbye. She said she was going to take him from me." And then I broke down, sobbing like crazy.

"She can't do that," Caitlin told me. Then she went on in words that were supposed to make me feel better. "Look, if I were you, I wouldn't worry about Justin so much. I think you've got to stop Danni from pushing you around like that."

"I know. The last thing I need is to have Danni start bullying me again. What should I do?"

"Maybe you should try to talk to her. Tell her that you're not going to put up with it. You know what they say, you have to stand up to bullies."

"You think so?"

"I know so," Caitlin replied. "Just keep your cool and explain the whole thing. I mean, it can't hurt to be nice. Then she'll have no excuse to be mean to you. And at least she'll know how you feel."

"You're right. I'll try to talk to her tomorrow," I said. After all, Danni hadn't *always* been a bully. Maybe if we just talked it all out, then it would all work out. Maybe it would all come out just fine.

CHAPTER 4

Talking and Whispering

It seems foolish now, but the next morning I woke up with a smile on my face. Talking to Danni had to make things better, I thought. After all, we were both older and more mature, weren't we? We weren't little kids any more.

As I walked to school I thought back to when I was friends with Danni. The more I remembered, the more I could see why Danni acted the way she did.

I used to hate going to Danni's house to play. Someone was always yelling over there. If Danni's parents weren't yelling at her for something, they were busy yelling at each other. Her mom would call her stepdad a bum and a loser. Once, the fighting got so bad that her stepdad threw a glass at her mom. It missed, but the glass hit the wall and shattered. After that, I always made sure Danni came over to my house to play. I didn't want to get mixed up in her family fights.

Maybe if you grow up in a house like that, you just learn to be a bully. Maybe you learn to be mean just to survive.

I was still thinking about Danni when I got to school. I was scared to talk to her but I wanted to get it over with. So I walked straight to the parking lot where all the smokers hung out. I saw Danni right away. She was standing there, smoking with three other girls. All of them were wearing tight jeans and tight tops.

Before I could open my mouth to speak, Danni saw me. "I didn't know they were having band practice out here today," she said.

The other girls looked at me and giggled. I guess my being in the band was one more thing that made me a loser — at least for them.

I decided to ignore what she said. I took a deep breath. "Danni, I was wondering if I could talk to you about something."

"I have nothing to say to *you*, Ms. Rat" she replied, walking up to me and blowing smoke in my face. "You got something you want to say to me?"

Right away, I knew that talking to Danni was a real bad idea. She had all her friends with her, and I had no one. I backed up a step. The words came tumbling out of my mouth.

"I . . . I . . . uh, just wanted to ask you to leave me and Justin alone," I stuttered. "I've never done anything to you." As soon as the words were out of my mouth, I knew how lame they sounded.

Her friends started laughing. Danni just stood there smiling. "Allie, you are *so-o-o-o* stupid. To start with, you've done plenty to me. But so what? As for your boyfriend, I can't help it if Justin thinks I'm hotter than you are."

"He does not," I shot back. My words came out sounding stupid.

"Listen, Allie, you've got two choices," Danni went on. "Either you let me have him or . . ."

"Or what?"

"You don't want to know about 'or what'" Danni said. Then she stomped out her smoke on the ground.

I couldn't say one more word. I felt like crying. All I wanted to do was clear things up between me and Danni, but she just wanted to hurt me.

I looked down at the ground. I looked at the crushed smoke. Then I looked up and saw Danni's cold eyes. She stared back — smug, powerful. I looked away.

At last, I turned around and walked back into the school. Behind me I could hear the girls laughing. I wished I could go home and never come back to school. One more time, I could feel tears in my eyes.

*　*　*

For almost a week, nothing happened. I started to relax. Maybe Caitlin was right — maybe it was enough to talk to Danni. Maybe she'd never follow through on her threats. Justin and I went out on Friday night, just like usual. My mom gave me the usual dirty look when I got home late, but I didn't care. I still had my boyfriend, and I still had my life. Maybe Danni Heller had just given up and moved on to some new victim.

But the next Monday, things started to go wrong. Someone wrote a big swear word on my binder. It was in magic marker, so I couldn't get it off. Later that day, there was a note stuffed into my locker. "Give him up," was all the note said. I knew just who had put it there.

On Wednesday, it got worse. It began in math class, just before the lesson began. When the class was almost full, I heard a guy call my name. "Hey, Allie," he said in a joking voice. "How about I call you tonight? I hear you're available."

It was Dave Berton, one of the sleaziest guys in the school. He was always trying to get girls to go for rides in his car, but nobody would. Not all guys are out for one thing, but Dave sure was.

What made it worse was the fact that I didn't even know the guy. I didn't think Dave knew my name, never mind my phone number.

What was going on? I looked around at the rest of the class. A few people were laughing. A few more were staring at me. They acted as if Dave had every right to say something like that.

Danni was in my math class and had just sat down. She was laughing harder than the rest. "Who would think *you'd* be a girl like that," she said to me. "What's Justin going to think once he finds out?"

"What are you talking about?" I asked.

"Nothing," she said. "Just a joke in the guys' john."

I turned around. What kind of joke about me would be in the guys' bathroom? I had to find out somehow.

A kid named Greg Parsons was sitting beside me. I didn't know Greg that well, but he had helped me with some math problems a few times. Plus he was the only guy in the class not laughing at me. I decided to ask him for some help.

"Greg?" I whispered.

He looked up and smiled. "Yeah?"

"Look, this is going to sound a little weird, but listen. Danni said there was some kind of joke in the guys' bathroom. Would you check it out for me?"

"Sure, I'll do it after class," he said. "I'll meet you at your locker and let you know."

I should have felt better when Greg offered to help. But something else was nagging at me. Behind me, beside me, the kids were whispering. I couldn't hear them, really. I couldn't catch more than a word or two. But somehow I knew that the whispers were about me.

CHAPTER 5

April Is the Cruelest Month

After what felt like a few thousand years, the buzzer rang and class was over. I grabbed my books and was first out the door. I didn't want anyone else speaking to me until I knew what the joke was about.

I headed straight to my locker and waited for Greg. While I was waiting, Caitlin came up to me.

"What's wrong, Allie?" she asked. One look at my face and she knew I was in trouble. "It looks like you've seen Freddy Kreuger coming down the hall."

"It's worse," I told her. "The truth is I don't know what's wrong. Everyone was laughing at me in math class. Then Danni said something about a joke in the boys' bathroom. And then all the whispering started."

"So what are you going to do?" Caitlin asked, looking as worried as she sounded.

"I got Greg Parsons to go into the bathroom to check it out. I'm just waiting for him to tell me the bad news."

"I'm sure it can't be *that* awful," she replied. "Besides, nobody pays attention to stuff written in the bathroom. I mean, how stupid do you think guys are?"

Just then, Greg came out of the bathroom and walked towards us. From the look on his face, I knew he had bad news.

"You sure you want to know about this, Allie?" he asked. Greg was looking down at the floor. "It's just something stupid — the janitors will wipe it off tonight."

"What did it say?" I snapped.

"Well, I won't give you the graphic stuff," Greg replied. "It kind of suggested that you, uh, do lots of stuff with lots of guys."

"That is *so-o-o-o* stupid!" Caitlin spat out.

"The trouble is, there's a phone number — 555-2134.'"

I took in a deep breath. That was my phone number. Caitlin put her hand on my back, trying to comfort me.

The three of us stood there, awkwardly. I felt

like crying; Caitlin was trying to make me feel better; Greg looked upset at the whole thing.

Greg was the first of us to speak. "Allie, if it makes you feel any better, nobody will believe a word of it. That kind of garbage gets written all the time. I'll go talk to the custodians and make sure they clean it off."

"Thanks, Greg," I said, but it didn't make me feel much better.

"Look I gotta get to my next class. But if any of the guys ask, I'll tell them it's just a stupid joke," said Greg. "Any guy who makes something of it, well, I'll just punch him out."

That made Caitlin smile. Greg was a great guy, but he was only about five feet tall. Still, it was nice that *somebody* was willing to stick up for me.

Gregg left and I tried to hold it together — really I did. But then the tears came up from some-place deep inside, and I started to cry.

"What are you going to do?" Caitlin asked.

"I don't know. What guy would write something like that about me? And what's Justin going to think if he hears about it?"

"If Justin really cares about you, he'll know it's a lie," Caitlin replied. "He won't believe something stupid that's written on a bathroom wall."

Suddenly the buzzer rang for our next class.

"Are you going to be okay?" Caitlin asked. "We can skip class and just go hang out or something."

I couldn't believe that Caitlin was offering to skip class. She was a straight-A student and had never missed a class in her life.

"No, I'll be all right," I said. "But I'll walk home with you tonight, okay?"

"Deal," she said and then rushed off.

I slumped down the hall to my English class. I kept my eyes straight ahead, trying to show people that I was *above* any scribbles on a bathroom wall. In a couple of hours, the marker would be gone. It would all be history. For now, I just had to keep under control.

"Glad you could make it, Allie," said Ms. Drayton when I opened the classroom door. She smiled at me even though I was late. "Go grab a seat."

There was only one desk left at the back of the

classroom, so I started walking towards it. I passed two guys who looked at me and then started giggling. It was sleazy Dave and a friend of his — two real losers. I tried to ignore them.

I had a hard time paying attention to what was going on. I kept feeling the eyes of the others on me. And I could hear the whispers, always followed by a dirty laugh.

A girl that hung around with Danni walked by my desk and dropped a note in front of me. There were only two words on it. "Justin knows," it said.

I sucked in a breath. I didn't know if she was handing me the note to be helpful or to make me feel worse. I had a hunch Justin would find out sooner or later, but I wanted to talk to him before he saw the writing.

Ms. Drayton cut into my thoughts. "Do I not bleed?" I heard Ms. Drayton say. We were studying *The Merchant of Venice*. "Isn't Shylock telling us that words can hurt as much as a physical wound?" she asked. There were no answers, because it was a simple truth.

I now knew how much they really could hurt.

When class was finally over for the day, I looked for Justin. He wasn't at his locker and he wasn't waiting at mine. I started to worry. It wasn't like him to not meet up with me after school. Justin still hadn't come to my locker by the time I had all my books in my backpack. I waited around for a few more minutes but he never showed.

As I was leaving school, Caitlin came up beside me. "Survive the day?" she asked.

"Kind of," I told her. "But now Justin isn't here so I think . . . well . . . "

"He's a good guy, Allie," Caitlin told me. "Even if he saw what they wrote, he wouldn't believe it. He might even punch out the guy who did it."

"The guy or girl," I corrected her.

"Yeah, right," Caitlin replied.

April is the cruelest month — some poet wrote that, too. Last month, in March, everything at school was different. I had good marks, a cool English teacher and hardly a care in the world. I had a couple of good friends who liked me and a boyfriend who loved me, or so I thought. And now . . .

"Did you see Justin at school today?" I asked Caitlin.

"Yeah, I did, actually, but he didn't see me," she said. "He came out the front doors of the school about five minutes after the lunch bell. I waved to him but he just kept walking."

That didn't sound like my boyfriend. I quickly pulled out my cell phone and pressed his number — memory #1. His cell rang and rang, but there was no answer, so I left a message. "Hey, Justin, it's me. Look, maybe you heard about that garbage in school today, but I want to talk to you about it. Just give me a call, okay?"

I closed my phone and turned back to Caitlin. We were already standing in front of my house. "I guess I'll see you tomorrow," I said.

"Of course," Caitlin said. "But if you need someone to talk to tonight, I'll be at home, ok?"

My mom was sitting in the living room, waiting for me, when I came through the door. "You had a couple of calls," mom said.

"Justin?" I asked.

"No, a couple of other boys. They didn't leave

their names, but they sounded kind of giggly. Do all teenage boys giggle like little kids?"

"I . . . uh, I don't know," I said with a lump in my throat. "They didn't, uh, say why they were calling?"

"No," my mom replied, "I figured it was just some school thing."

I sucked in a breath to keep from bursting into tears. "Yeah, it's just a school thing," I replied. Then I turned and raced upstairs before my mom could ask me any more questions.

As I was on the stairs, I heard the phone ring and my mom answer it. "It's for you, Allie," she called up to me.

"Is it Justin?" I asked, my voice cracking.

"No, some other kid."

I picked up the phone, my hand trembling as I held it. At the other end was some heavy breathing, then a couple of swear words, and then a laugh.

I slammed the phone down and sat there, shaking. At last, I couldn't hold it back any longer. I started to cry. Why was this happening to *me*?

CHAPTER 6

Whispers

I woke up the next morning with a sick feeling in the pit of my stomach. I didn't want to face the kids at school. And I didn't want to talk to my parents downstairs.

"Allie, did you unplug the phone last night?" my mom asked at breakfast.

"Well, uh, maybe I knocked it off or something," I told her, lying through my teeth. "I'll go upstairs and check."

"Well, there's no dial tone. So I was kind of wondering," she replied.

My dad made a face as he stood by the coffee machine. "Of course, nobody ever call us. So how would we know?"

I squirmed a bit in my chair, then put down my spoon. "You know, mom, I'm really not feeling too good today. Do you think I could stay home?"

My brother started to laugh. My mom just shot me one of those looks. Nobody in our house could ever stay home. We could be dying in pain, groaning on the floor, and mom would still make us go to school.

"No, Allie," Mom replied. "Go fix the phone and get yourself ready to go. We're going to our jobs and you're going to school. It's as simple as that."

Oh, I wish it were that simple! Kids are whispering about me. Somebody is writing garbage about me in the washroom. Now a bunch of weird guys are calling my house. I knew that Danni had to be behind this, but she must have a whole gang to back her up.

Who did I have? Caitlin for sure . . . but Justin?

I trudged to school, carrying my flute under one arm. I felt sick — sick at heart — and maybe sick to my stomach. Danni and her gang were out to get me. That much I knew. What's worse, I knew they had only just begun.

When I got to my locker, I saw that they had struck again. Someone had written the word "SLUT" in bright pink nail polish across the door.

Ms. Drayton came out and stood beside me as I looked at the letters. Four letters. Why do so many swear words have just four letters?

"Don't worry, Allie," said Ms. Drayton. "We'll get somebody to clean it off. But do you have any idea who did this?"

"Uh, no," I lied, just as I had always lied. *I'm not a rat*, I told myself. *I'll find some way to deal with this myself.*

"Are you sure?" Ms. Drayton asked. From the look on her face, I knew she knew. "You don't have to deal with this alone, you know."

I shook my head. *I'm not a rat,* I repeated to myself. Whatever they did, I wouldn't rat out.

When I came into first class, I took the seat

closest to our math teacher. I figured no one could do anything to me there. I wasn't ready for the teacher to go running off to the office.

The second the teacher was gone, Danni came up beside me. She had a smirk on her face.

"Looks like someone marked up your locker," Danni said. She was tapping her fingers on my desk.

I didn't want to look her in the eye, so I looked at her hands. The nail polish was the same colour that was on my locker. Danni was waving her fingers right in front of my face. She was *bragging* about what she did.

"Aren't you going to say something, you little loser?" she said, whispering the last words.

"I don't have anything to say to you," I mumbled. Then I looked down at my math book. Danni shook her head and walked away.

Around me, all I could hear were whispers. Nobody stood up for me. Nobody told Danni to bug off. Nobody seemed to be on my side. Instead, there were whispers, words I couldn't quite hear. The kids were talking — and I was sure they were talking about me.

When it was time for lunch, I went looking for Justin. He wasn't at his locker so I headed into the lunch room. I saw him sitting with the guys from his basketball team.

He didn't see me at first, so I tapped him on the shoulder. "Justin? Can I talk to you?" I asked.

He turned around to look at me. Before all this, he would have smiled at me, maybe kissed me on the cheek. He'd give me the look that made me feel special. But today, he had a nervous look on his face. It was as if he was embarrassed that I was there.

I could hear some of the guys from his team laughing.

Dave Berton spoke up before Justin said a word. "Hey guys, look who's here! It's our very *favourite* girl!"

I blushed a bright red. I could catch the dirty meaning behind his words.

"Justin!" I repeated. My words came out angry — I couldn't help it.

"Oh, hey, Allie," Justin replied.

I just couldn't believe he was acting like this.

I needed to talk to him — seriously — right away. But Justin wasn't acting like my boyfriend. He was acting as if he barely knew me.

"Can we just *talk*," I asked, "by ourselves?" I tried to shoot an angry look at Dave and all his basketball buddies.

"Uh, maybe a little later," Justin said. A guy on his team was elbowing him. The rest of the guys were full-out laughing — at *me*.

Don't let these jerks see you break down, I told myself. *Don't let them see how this is getting to you.*

"I'll meet you at your locker after school," I said. "And Justin, just in case you didn't know, none of it's true. None of it!"

"*Ohhhhhhh*," I heard all the guys groan as I walked away.

CHAPTER 7

Dumped

After school, I waited by Justin's locker. I tried to ignore the kids who were looking at me. I didn't look at the guys who laughed and the girls who whispered. Inside, I wanted to die. Outside, I tried to look proud and in-control.

While I was waiting, Greg Parsons walked by. "Hey, Allie," he said, smiling at me. It was the first time someone had smiled at me all day.

"Hey," I said back.

I must have looked pretty sad. Greg stopped and touched my shoulder. "Don't worry about what some people are saying," he said. "I don't believe it and your real friends won't believe it either. That's what really matters, right?"

I looked up at him and smiled. I wondered how many *real* friends I had.

"Thanks, Greg," I said. "I just can't understand how something like this could spread so fast. I know Danni wants to get me, but the others?"

"Looks like Danny has her old gang together," Greg replied. "You're the target of the week. But don't worry, it will all pass." Then he looked down at his watch. "Listen, I have to go off to a student council meeting. But if you need a friend, Allie, I'm always here."

I watched Greg walk down the hall and thought about how nice he was. He wasn't tall or cool or hot like Justin, but he was nice. *Why wasn't Justin acting like Greg?* I wondered. *Why wasn't my own boyfriend protecting me from all this?*

I was still thinking about all that when Justin finally showed up at his locker.

"So, what do you want to talk about?" Justin asked. He didn't even say hi or look at me. He just started twirling the dial on his lock.

"You know what's been going on," I whispered. "You know that somebody is spreading rumours about me. You must know they're not true. So why have *you* been avoiding me?"

"I haven't been avoiding you," he replied. He looked sort of embarrassed, like he didn't want me around. It was like he hardly knew me. "I've just been, well, you know, like really busy."

Justin turned away from me. He opened his locker, grabbed his books and basketball clothes, and shoved them into his backpack.

I touched his shoulder and made him turn to look at me. I had to tell him. I had to tell him what I was thinking and what my heart was feeling.

"Justin, I've really needed you the last few days. People have been saying a lot of stuff about me and none of it's true. I need somebody to defend me, Justin. I need you. . . ." I wanted to tell him about the nail polish and the phone calls, but I couldn't get the words out. I was all choked up, and the words just wouldn't come.

"Let's talk outside," he said. Justin still wasn't looking at me. He just grabbed his bag and started for the door.

I followed after him. I felt like a little kid following after her dad at K-Mart. It was hopeless, and I knew it.

Outside, it was windy and wet. A few big drops of April rain had started to fall on the sidewalk in front of us. I wanted to grab Justin's hand and bring him to my house, but I didn't think he'd let me touch him. We walked for a few minutes, not speaking. We were both just staring straight ahead. At last, Justin stopped and looked down at me.

"Allie, I really loved dating you. We had lots of fun together . . ." he began.

This is the end, I said to myself. *He's breaking up with me — I can hear it in his voice.*

"But you don't want to be my boyfriend any more," I finished for him.

"It's not that . . . I really like you, but some of

the guys are talking." Now Justin was having trouble finding words.

"You *believe* the rumours?" I shot back. I started to get mad, but then my anger died away. It was all hopeless. "What are they saying anyway?"

"Just that you're kind of loose, you know? And Danni says she saw you with a couple of older guys."

"You believe *Danni*?"

"I don't know what I believe any more," he moaned. "I guess I'm not sure what kind of girl you really are."

That's when I lost it. They say that when you're pushed all the way down, when there's no hope left, that you finally come up fighting. I guess I had reached that point.

"After all this time, you don't know me?" I screamed. "You believe the dumb rumours from somebody like Danni Heller? You trust rumours more than you trust me?"

"Well, I don't know. It's just that some of the guys — "

I cut him off. I didn't care about *some of the*

guys, or what Justin *didn't know*. It was time to figure out who was on my side and who wasn't.

"Can't you see that Danni started it all? She started making moves on you, and when that didn't work she had to trash me. She was the one who wrote my number in the bathroom. She was the one who wrote on my locker. She's just using her old gang to spread stupid rumours!" I blurted out the words all at once.

Justin looked at me but said nothing.

And I had nothing left. Suddenly I felt very afraid and very alone. I wanted so badly for Justin to believe me. I wanted everything to go back the way it was.

"Why would Danni go to all that trouble?" he asked at last.

"For you, you big jerk," I spat out. "And because she hates me."

The heavy rain drops started to turn into a downpour. I pulled up the hood of my jacket and listened to the rain fall on it.

Justin shook his head and looked down at me. "I don't believe you, Allie. There are just too many people saying things." Justin paused before he delivered the line I feared most. "I — I don't think we should see each other any more."

I knew it was coming, but it still felt like my heart was falling into my stomach. I sucked in air and let out a big sob.

I couldn't stand it any more. I didn't want to cry in front of Justin. I didn't want him to know how much he meant to me, not after the way he treated me. So I started running down the street. There was a loud crash of thunder and I thought I heard Justin call my name. But I just kept running. Somehow, some way, I had to fix all this. Somehow I had to show them all.

CHAPTER 8

Caitlin's Idea

The next morning, I felt even worse than the day before. I didn't want to go to school and face the kids. I felt sick about losing Justin because of a bunch of lies. I felt stupid because almost all of my "friends" were treating me like trash.

I hid my head under the pillow until my mom came in the room. "Allie?" she said, opening my door.

"Yeah, I know Mom. I'm getting up," I sighed.

"Listen, I came to tell you that Caitlin's waiting for you downstairs. She said she needed to talk to you."

I sat up in bed, then raced around my room to get ready for school. After throwing on some clothes and running a brush through my hair, I went downstairs.

"Wow, that was fast," Caitlin said when she saw me.

"Well, I don't have a boyfriend to impress, do I?" I had told Caitlin all about it when I got home from school. She was the only one who could understand.

"Let's not talk about it right now," said Caitlin. She shot a look at my mom.

We had just got out the door when I let loose. "I can't stand this, Caitlin. I'm dumped and bullied and whispered about. I only have one friend left and I feel like . . . "

"Stop!" Caitlin ordered. She turned and looked at me. "Allie, you have to talk to someone about this. It's too big for you and too big for me. We need some help."

I sighed and nodded. Caitlin was right, of course.

"I was thinking about it last night," Caitlin went on. "You know that Danni is behind it, so all you have to do is go to a teacher and tell them what's happening."

"And end up being a rat?" I shot back. "I'm sure that would make me popular."

"Allie, get real. Even if you look like a wuss for telling a teacher, at least the bullying will stop. At this point, you don't have much left to lose."

I sighed. "Who do you think I should talk to?" I asked.

"Well, you can't go to the principal; he's a jerk. And that would make it too big a deal," said Caitlin, thinking out loud. "I think you need to go to someone you can trust. You need someone that Danni will listen to, because you and Danni need to sit down and talk."

"I already tried that," I reminded her. "Danni doesn't exactly like to chat."

"I know," Caitlin replied. "That's why you have to get a teacher on side. That way Danni *has* to talk."

"It sounds lame," I said.

"Yeah, I know, but you really have no choice. What else can you do — transfer schools, pray that people forget, jump off a bridge?"

She was right, again. The last thing I wanted to do was go to a teacher, but there wasn't really any other way to stop all this.

When I got to school, there was a bunch of girls outside, pointing at me and laughing. I just looked down, but Caitlin grabbed my hand. "Hold your head up, Allie," she said as we walked past the group. "We're going to fight back and beat this."

I made up my mind right then. I didn't want to dread going to school every day. I didn't want to worry that someone was going to call me a name. I didn't want to be afraid that someone would write something on my locker. I needed some help.

When Caitlin and I had put our stuff in our lockers, I turned to her. "I'm going to ask Ms. Drayton what I should do about the bullying," I said.

Caitlin smiled and gave me a big hug. "That's great, Allie. It'll be hard, but I know you'll feel better once you talk to her. Do you want me to come with you?" she asked.

"Could you?"

"Of course! I'll meet you in front of Ms. Drayton's room at lunch."

The rest of the morning seemed to drag, mostly because I was dreading talking to Ms. Drayton about my problems. I mean, it's hard to admit to a teacher that you're being bullied. It makes you feel like a loser.

Ms. Drayton's English class was my second class of the day, right after math. When I sat down and saw Ms. Drayton smiling at me, I felt a little better. Of all my teachers, she was the one I could talk to.

When the class was over I waited outside the classroom door for Caitlin. About ten minutes later she showed up, out of breath. "Sorry, Allie," she said. "I tried to get here as fast as I could but I had to stay back and get some help with my history project."

"Don't worry about it," I said. "I'm in no rush to do this."

Caitlin rolled her eyes. "Come on, Allie, let's get it over with," she said. Then she grabbed my arm and dragged me into the classroom.

Ms. Drayton was still sitting at her desk marking some papers. She didn't seem to notice us come in. "Ms. Drayton?" Caitlin asked.

She looked up and smiled. "The dynamic duo," she said. "What's up?"

Both of us were silent for a minute. Caitlin looked at me waiting for me to say something, but I was too embarrassed.

"We wanted to talk to you about something," Caitlin started since I wasn't about to. "Maybe you've heard — there've been some rumours about Allie going around. We . . . uh, we need help stopping them."

I felt my face get hot so I looked down, away from both of them.

Ms. Drayton set down her pen and motioned for us to grab some chairs. "Why don't you two sit down and tell me about it," she said. "Allie, what is this all about?"

It felt as if my tongue was stuck in my throat. Why was it so hard to say the truth? Why couldn't I just tell the story?

"Is somebody picking on you?" she asked.

My tongue was still frozen. I felt like I wanted to throw up. But finally a single word came out. "Yes," I whispered. "It's Danni . . . Danni Heller!"

And then the tears began. I cried and shook and coughed and cried some more. Ms. Drayton just waited until I was done. She kept waiting while I told her everything. Everything.

When I was all done, Ms. Drayton didn't say

anything for a few minutes. She seemed to be thinking about what to do. "I'm glad you guys came and told me about this," she began. "You shouldn't have to deal with bullying like this on your own."

"What do you think we should do?" Caitlin asked.

Ms. Drayton thought for a second. She looked at both of us before she spoke. "I think the first thing I need to do is have a meeting with Allie and Danni and their parents. They need to know what's going on. Even if Danni isn't behind the stuff that's being written, she is bullying you in other ways. That needs to stop."

I took in a deep breath. "I haven't told my parents about this," I said.

I thought Ms. Drayton would be surprised, but she wasn't. "Not many kids do tell their parents. It's like a nasty secret, even if it's not your fault. But, Allie, you really must tell them tonight. Nobody can help you unless you speak up yourself."

"I guess," I sighed.

"You tell them I want to arrange a meeting and I'll call your house later."

When we got out of the classroom I felt relieved. "That wasn't so bad, I guess," I said to Caitlin.

"I told you it wouldn't be," she replied.

"Now all I have to do is tell my parents," I said. There was a lump in my throat even thinking about that.

CHAPTER 9

This Had Better Work

When I got home that afternoon, both my mom and dad were in the house. Just my luck, I thought. It's easier to handle them one at a time. The one day I have to have a serious talk and they're both home early.

"Hey honey," my mom said. She poked her head around the door of the kitchen. "Your father and I thought we'd catch a movie tonight. We're cooking up dinner a bit early."

"Okay," I mumbled. I set my knapsack down just as my dad walked into the front hall.

"I thought you'd be happy to get rid of us," he joked, "After all, you get the whole house to yourself tonight. Now that those phone calls have stopped, you might even have a quiet night."

I looked up at my dad and took a deep breath. "There's something I need to talk to you about. You and mom," I blurted out.

My dad looked worried. "It sounds serious," he said. "I'll go get your mom." My father has never been good with sitting down and talking. He must have been worried I was going to tell him I was pregnant or something.

When my mom came out into the hall, she looked really worried. "What is it Allie? What's the problem?"

"I . . . I've got to tell you something," I began. And for the second time that day I spilled my guts. When I was finished, they both looked angry.

"I've got a mind to go over to that Danni's house and tell her father just what kind of kid he has," said my dad.

"Have you talked to any teachers about this?" asked my mom. She ignored my dad's plan.

"I was just getting to that," I said. "I talked to Ms. Drayton today and she thinks all of us should have a meeting. It will be me, Danni, you two and Danni's parents."

"Sounds good to me," my dad said, clenching his fists. "I'll let her old man know what's what."

My mom looked at my dad and just shook her head. "Frank, I don't think starting a fight with

73

Danni's father is going to solve much. And you talk so much tougher than you really are."

Just then the phone rang. My mom went out to the kitchen and picked it up. She waited for a second to see if it was another crank call. There was a pause. Then she said, "Yes, this is Allie's mom."

I knew she was talking to Ms. Drayton. "Yes . . . she just finished telling me all about it," my mom went on. "You've talked to Danni's mom as well?"

This had better work, I thought to myself. If I wasn't a loser before, having a teacher call someone else's parents would make me a total reject.

"Tomorrow at 4:30 sounds great," I heard my mom say. When she got off the phone, she came back into the living room and gave me a big hug. "Everything's going to be okay, Allie," she told me. "A little talk and this should be all cleared up."

I think I had heard that line once before.

* * *

I called Caitlin that night and she answered after the first ring.

"I thought it might be you," she said when she picked up the phone. "So how did the talk with your parents go?"

"Fine, I guess. We're having that parent-teacher meeting tomorrow after school," I sighed.

"It won't be that bad," Caitlin said. "After all, what can Danni do when there's a bunch of adults on your side?"

"I'm not worried about what she's going to do in the meeting. I'm worried about afterwards," I said. "She's mean," I said, "and her gang is scary."

"Your mom can be pretty scary when she gets mad," Caitlin said. "I don't think Danni will mess around with you if your mom has anything to say to her."

I smiled. My mom was a lot tougher than my father. She could get the truth out of anyone. I hope Danni would just admit to what she did. I hoped that she'd promise to stop.

While I was thinking about all this, Caitlin asked me a question out of the blue. "So what do you think of Greg Parsons?"

"Huh?" I asked, a little confused.

"You know, the little guy who went spying in the bathroom for you. The not-bad-looking guy who was super nice to you just a couple of days ago?"

"I know who he *is*, Caitlin."

"So-o-o-o . . . what do you think of him?" she asked again.

"Why do you want know?" I said.

"Just wondering . . ."

"Come on, just tell me why you're asking."

"Well Greg was asking me about you today. He heard what happened between you and Justin and he wanted to find out if you were okay," Caitlin blurted out.

"Really?" I asked. I felt my heart skip a beat and my face got hot. After all, Greg was pretty cute and he *had* been really nice to me lately.

"So, if you ask me, I think he's got the hots for you," Caitlin said.

"Right now, I'd be lucky if a slug had the hots for me," I told her.

"If that's what you want to believe, Allie, then go ahead. But trust me — Greg is interested, and he is kind of cute," she said.

"Well, I have a few other things to think about right now."

"Fair enough," Caitlin admitted. "I'm changing the subject. But life goes on when this mess with Danni is over. Right?"

Of course she was right. But the mess with Danni wasn't over yet. I had no way of knowing what would happen at the meeting. Would it fix the problem, or just make my life worse?

CHAPTER 10

The Class and the Meeting

The next day, Caitlin met me at my house first thing. We walked to school together and talked about everything else — everything but the meeting. I think we both knew what was coming.

I was dreading first class. It was Ms. Drayton's English class, one of the classes I had with Danni and her gang. It was quiet when I got to the door. Then, as I walked past Danni to get to my seat, she whispered something. A girl looked up at me and started laughing.

Almost as soon as the laughter came out of their mouths, I heard a loud voice. "That's enough!" I turned and saw Ms. Drayton glaring at the two girls.

Ms. Drayton looked around at the rest of the class. The kids sat there, stunned and silent. There are teachers who yell and it's no big deal, Ms. Drayton wasn't one of them. I don't think we had ever heard Ms. Drayton raise her voice before. Maybe that's why her words came as such a surprise.

At last, Ms. Drayton broke the silence. "I'd like to thank Danni for helping me launch into today's discussion."

"What's that?" Danni shot back.

"Bullying," Ms. Drayton said. "Bullying with words, not with fists." She paused to let her words sink in. "Okay, here's my first question. Who here thinks they're smart?"

Everyone, even some pretty dumb kids, raised their hands.

"So I see we're all smart people," Ms. Drayton went on. She walked up and down the aisles, staring at all of us.

"Next question. Who here believes things that are written on bathroom walls?"

As soon as she said this, my face turned red. I looked down at my desk. A few guys snickered. No one raised a hand.

"Well, I'm glad that no one is that dumb. We've all figured out something simple. What you read on a wall isn't a good source of information." Ms. Drayton waited. "Let's face it, people who hang out in a bathroom must have some kind of problem. People who spread rumours need to get a life, right?" She stared at each face in the room. "I mean, who would waste their time doing something like that?"

A bunch of kids looked over at Danni and began to laugh. For the first time, Danni seemed upset. She looked down and pretended to do work.

"It's funny how a few nasty words can make some people feel more powerful. But deep down, deep down," she repeated, "they have a problem. They're bullies!"

A few girls who were Danni's friends began looking at her. Maybe they were thinking of things that she had done to them.

"So what do we do with bullies?" asked Ms. Drayton. "To start with, we can't let bullies get away with what they do. If all of us just got together and told the bully to get lost, there would be no bullying. I know this sounds simple, but it works. Now let me tell you *why* it works. . . ."

By the end of the class, many of the kids were glaring at Danni. It wasn't that Mrs. Drayton even used Danni's name, but we all knew. We all knew who the bully was. And most of the kids knew that I was the chosen victim.

Danni just pretended to ignore it all, but I could tell she was nervous. When the buzzer rang at the end of class, it wasn't soon enough for her.

I kept my eye on Danni as she left the room. She tried to talk to Dave Berton outside, but he just gave her a look. She went to a couple of her friends, but they turned aside. I guess Ms. Drayton's talk had some effect.

The rest of the day flew by. The whispering

stopped. The pointing fingers were aimed at Danni, not me. I think word of Ms. Drayton's talk had gone around. She was a popular teacher. What she said and how she felt made a difference.

When four thirty finally came, I met my mom and dad outside school. Together, we went to Ms. Drayton's classroom. I was surprised to see that Danni was already there. She was there by herself.

"Neither of my folks could make it tonight," Danni told Ms. Drayton.

"Why's that?" I heard Ms. Drayton ask as we walked into the room. She didn't sound as if she believed Danni.

At that moment, they saw me and my parents.

When Danni saw us, the look on her face turned from sadness to anger.

In a second, her nasty mouth was back. "My parents aren't here because they're busy. Maybe I don't have a family like little Miss Perfect," she said. Her eyes were angry. "Are you guys happy now? My mom couldn't make it because she's working overtime at her crappy job. And my stepdad? He's in jail. Is that good enough for you? Does that make you feel happy?"

All of us just stared at her. I knew about Danni's family, but I don't think my mom or Ms. Drayton did. Danni's face was hard and cold.

"That's fine, Danni," Ms. Drayton said. She put her hand on Danni's shoulder and tried to make her feel better. Danni shrugged it off.

"I guess we all know what this is about," Ms. Drayton began. "Maybe we can start with the writing in the bathroom. Danni, do you have anything you want to say?"

There was a long pause. I could hear the clock ticking and my own breathing. Danni looked at Ms. Drayton, at her nails, at me, then down at the floor.

"Danni?" Ms. Drayton asked again.

"I did it, okay?" she said. "You already know that, don't you? You knew it was me all along. I got a guy to sneak into the washroom with me . . . I used the nail polish . . . "

There was more silence in the room, so thick you could cut it with a knife.

"I'm just so sick of Allie," Danni went on. "Allie

and her Miss Perfect life. I wanted her boyfriend. . .
I wanted her life."

Did Danni begin to sob? I heard a big intake of
breath, and then she turned her face away from me.
If Danni was going to cry, it wouldn't be in front of
me.

Again, there was silence. I don't think my
mother knew what to say, and I sure didn't. Finally
Ms. Drayton spoke to Danni in a quiet voice.

"Danni, I want you to come back and talk to
me first thing tomorrow. Right now I'm going to

talk to Allie's mom and dad. Why don't both of you girls wait outside?"

When we were outside the classroom, it was pretty awkward. I looked down the hall. Danni took a Kleenex and wiped her eyes. At last, Danni said something. "Look, Allie, I didn't mean it," she began.

"Apology accepted," I said, looking at the floor. I was still angry with her. Yes, I felt sorry for her, but the anger was still there.

"Maybe one day we could be friends again?" she asked. "I mean, we used to have so much fun as kids."

"I don't know Danni," I said. And I really didn't. She had messed up a lot of things in my life in just a few days. I had lost Justin and spent every night for the past week crying. I wasn't ready to be friends.

"Well, I hope you'll think about it," she said. She looked at me and smiled a half-smile, then turned and walked away. She was alone.

CHAPTER 11

Sticks and Stones

Rumours don't last long. A day after Danni got off my case, they began to disappear. They were old news. Once Danni stopped calling me names, nobody else did either.

Sticks and stones may break my bones,
But names will never hurt me.

But names do hurt. Being called a slut is a terrible thing. It gets worse if your boyfriend believes it. It gets worse still when your phone rings in the middle of the night and some strange guy gives you a dirty laugh. And it gets terrible when all the kids begin talking behind your back.

How does it start? With a whisper.

But what began in a week died off in a week. There were other things to think about — the school play, our band concert, tests and exams. By May, the sun was shining outside. Maybe it was shining inside my life, too. I was only missing one thing.

One day at the end of the month, Justin came up to my locker after school. He had that old look on his face, the one that said I was pretty special. It was the kind of look I used to love. It was the look I would have died for even a week ago, but now things were different.

"Hey, Allie," he began, "I guess you heard that I broke up with Danni."

"Sorry, Justin," I told him. "I don't listen to rumours — unlike some people."

"Well, I was kind of wondering . . . you know, there's this cool movie opening on Friday . . ."

He didn't have a chance to finish. Greg Parsons

was walking down the hall and stopped right beside me. He looked up at both Justin and me, but he didn't back away.

"Hey, Allie, are you heading home right now?" Greg asked. "'Cause if you are I could walk with you."

"Well, I . . . uh . . . "

I looked back and forth between Greg and Justin. I had to make a choice. There was this short student council guy and this tall, handsome basketball star. But I knew who had stuck by me that awful April. I knew who I could trust when things were looking bad. So the choice was simple.

"Sorry, Justin, but I'm going to be *real* busy on Friday," I told him. Then I turned to my friend. "Hey, Greg, let's get out of here."